Daisy and Delilah

— A Journey to Friendship —

Sydney Kaul

Archway Publishing books may be ordered through booksellers or by contacting:

Archway Publishing
1663 Liberty Drive
Bloomington, IN 47403
www.archwaypublishing.com
844-669-3957

Because of the dynamic nature of the Internet, any web addresses or links contained in
this book may have changed since publication and may no longer be valid. The views
expressed in this work are solely those of the author and do not necessarily reflect the views
of the publisher, and the publisher hereby disclaims any responsibility for them.

Any people depicted in stock imagery provided by Getty Images are models,
and such images are being used for illustrative purposes only.
Certain stock imagery © Getty Images.

ISBN: 978-1-6657-3310-6 (sc)
ISBN: 978-1-6657-3309-0 (hc)
ISBN: 978-1-6657-3311-3 (e)

Print information available on the last page.

Archway Publishing rev. date: 12/08/2022

ARCHWAY
PUBLISHING

DEDICATION PAGE

To my real-life dog and cat, Daisy and Luca, who were the inspiration for this book. I would also like to dedicate this to the children at the YMCA daycare whom I read to and hope to instill a love of reading and literature.

After a long day of school, Peyton came home and opened the door, where she found her yellow lab, Daisy already waiting. Daisy came bouncing towards her, squealing, and wagging her tail. Daisy jumped onto Peyton and licked her face excitedly.

"Come on Daisy, do you want to go for a walk?" Peyton asked her four-legged best friend. Daisy was already at the door with her leash in her mouth.

There is my favorite pond. Let's go swimming!

Peyton took Daisy off her leash and Daisy darted for the water.

Yay. I love to swim. It's refreshing, I can splash around, I can get that stick floating over there. "Daisy, come. That's enough now. It's time to go home." Peyton called Daisy.

"Daisy, cheese! Come and I'll give you some cheese," shouted Peyton.

Cheese! I'm coming, wait don't leave, hold on, here I come!

And Daisy came sprinting out of the pond.

Peyton fed Daisy her dinner, and then they sat on the couch together. Daisy nestled up close against Peyton's body, with Peyton occasionally scratching her belly. Daisy loved Peyton. She was stuck to her side like glue whenever Peyton was home.

The next morning after breakfast, Peyton gathered her things and said "Bye Daisy. I'm going to school now. Be a good girl. Here's your bone." Peyton closed the door and Daisy ran to the window to watch as she left the house.

Gosh, I hate when she leaves. I hate when I'm alone in the house. It's so boring and quiet.

"What do you mean no one is home? I'm here. Hello?! Don't I count? Way to hurt someone's feelings, geez," said Bone.

"You know what I mean," Daisy said.

"No, nope, I don't," said Bone, all sad.

"You can't play with me. You can't even move unless I pick you up," said Daisy as she scooped up Bone in her mouth.

Daisy put Bone down next to her on the bed, determined to sleep until Peyton returned.

"Come on, don't be so dramatic. There are other things you could do other than sleep," said Bone.

"It's just not fun. I really would like a friend here so I can play during the day, but I'll try," Daisy replied.

So, for the rest of the day, Daisy attempted to amuse herself. She looked out the window, she picked through the garbage, she pulled a pair of Peyton's dirty socks out of the hamper and chewed it. Finally, she chewed a pink blanket.

After all this, she looked at the clock. 11 am. "11 am!? It's only 11 am. That's it. I want a friend!" barked Daisy.

"Well how exactly are you going to get Peyton to bring home a friend for you?" asked Bone.

"Hmmm. I could show her how sad I am without a friend," Daisy replied

For the next couple of days, Daisy just laid around the house. Not playing, not wagging her tail, no whining for her walks. She didn't even eat the cheese Peyton offered.

"What's the matter Daisy? Why are you so sad?" Peyton asked as she pet Daisy's head.

Peyton knew something was wrong. She decided to take Daisy to play with her two best friends, Mabel and Moose. Peyton could see how much happier Daisy was with her friends.

Then one day, Peyton and her mother were passing by a pet store and there were some kittens in the window. Peyton had a great idea.

"Can we buy a cat? I know you said no to a dog, but cats are no trouble," suggested Peyton desperately.

After some convincing, Peyton came home with a friend for Daisy. "Daisy, I'm home. I have a surprise for you," Peyton called.

Daisy came barreling down the stairs. *Oh boy, oh boy. What could it be?*

Daisy looked around, confused. *Where? Where is my surprise? Wait. In that teeny, tiny case?* Daisy thought to herself.

Daisy peered inside the case and there she saw a cat. A CAT!

9

"NO!! This cannot be my new best friend. This is a cat. Peyton made a mistake. I am a dog. I absolutely cannot be best friends with a cat. WE are not the same. It just won't work," Daisy whined to Bone.

Peyton opened the case to introduce them to each other. Daisy and Delilah looked at one another and stared for a moment, both confused with how to act. Then, Daisy rushed over to sniff Delilah, but Delilah became fearful and hissed at Daisy, scurrying under the chair.

Daisy walked away unhappy and disappointed.

"They brought home a cat. A cat," she said to Bone.

"How am I supposed to be friends with a cat? I can't play with a cat. We are so different. Did you see how she hissed at me? I can't be friends with a cat. No way. Uh, uh. I refuse," Daisy said in a huff.

"Well, you are different. It's not as easy to be friends with a cat as it would a dog. And she did hiss at you. But she could have been afraid. And just because you are different doesn't mean you can't be friends. Why don't you try and play with Delilah?" Bone suggested.

"I guess I could give it a try," Daisy said reluctantly.

The next morning, Daisy approached Delilah, wagging her tail excitedly. Daisy tried playing chase. Daisy loved to play chase. It was one of her favorite games. She ran over to Delilah eagerly barking to get her attention and then ran away.

"Come on Delilah, try and get me. I bet you can't get me," squealed Daisy.

Delilah became frightened and ran under the couch to hide. Daisy ran to the couch and looked underneath for Delilah. She could see her, but she could not reach her. Daisy was determined to catch Delilah and win this game. She squatted down on her belly. She squeezed her paws under the couch. She almost made it, but she got stuck.

"What are you thinking? Look at you! You can't fit under there. You are far too big. Now come out before you get stuck permanently," Bone cautioned, holding back laughter.

"Ha. I'm smarter than you. And you are so silly thinking you could fit under the couch," Delilah remarked, secretly relieved that she was safe.

Embarrassed and sad, Daisy wiggled out from under the couch.

Bone could see she was upset and said, "Hey there's your rope, try playing tug of war."

"This is a great game. You will love it; I just know you will," she happily said as she dropped the rope at Delilah's feet.

"Why would I want to do that? That is the silliest game I've ever heard." Delilah walked away annoyed.

Delilah decided it was time to play some of her favorite games.

"Enough with these dog games," she rudely said. Delilah walked to the window where the string from the blinds was hanging. She jumped up and swatted at the string. The string swayed back and forth and back and forth. Delilah continued to swat at it, trying to catch it.

Daisy watched her and could not believe it. She walked right up to the string and grabbed it in one try.

Holding the string in her mouth, she says "are you just trying to catch it?" "This is not a fun game," grumbled Daisy.

"Well, it's not now, you just ruined it," purred Delilah.

Delilah then stealthily walked over to the dishwasher and started to play with the buttons. She pushed one button; it lit up and buzzed. She pushed another button and then another. Lights flashing and buzzing, she was having the best time entertaining herself.

Confused and frustrated, Daisy said "This is not a game. We can't play this together. You are just doing this by yourself."

"I know, let's go to the kitchen. There are always fun things to play with on the table," Delilah responded.

"Oh, this should be good." Bone said sarcastically.

On the kitchen table, Delilah saw a pen. She knocked the pen off the table onto the floor. She then swiped the pen on the floor, and it slid under the refrigerator. Then, she knocked off a pair of eyeglasses. Boom. The glasses landed on the floor. Delilah chased the eyeglasses. This time, it got stuck under the oven.

"Come on and play with these things I've knocked off the table," Delilah coaxed Daisy.

"No. These are Peyton's things. She will not like it at all. You could ruin them, and you already lost her pen under the fridge," said Daisy, worried.

"You are such a goody two shoes," Delilah said mockingly.

As the day went by, Daisy and Delilah struggled more and more to become friends. They could not find a way to have fun together. They just did not like the same games.

"Come on guys. There must be something you both like to do. Don't give up yet," Bone said encouragingly.

Daisy agreed with Bone and looked out the window. Just then an idea came to her. *I've got it! We can go outside and dig holes.*

As a last attempt to be friends, Daisy waddled over to Delilah. "Let's go outside," she suggested.

Delilah, intrigued with the outside world, agreed to follow Daisy. She had never been outside. She also saw birds and squirrels in the yard. Delilah was extremely excited.

"Hey, wait! Don't forget to bring me. Guys. Hello?" Bone shouted as they both hopped out of the doggy door, leaving Bone inside.

Daisy leapt and frolicked around the yard. Delilah carefully stepped one paw at a time, nervous and cautious of her surroundings. Daisy began to dig a hole. She dug with all her might and attention.

While Daisy's head was facing the ground, concentrated on her hole, Delilah snuck away underneath the fence, curious as to what lay beyond.

The hole Daisy was digging was quite large at this point. She stopped for a moment to admire it. She looked over to check on Delilah's progress. Not only did she realize Delilah was not digging a hole, but she was gone completely! Daisy looked all around the yard, but Delilah was nowhere in sight.

Daisy was irritated at first that Delilah was gone and wasn't watching her expertly dig a hole or digging one herself. She became less irritated but glad Delilah was gone when she realized her attempts at playing together had failed. She did not want to be friends with a cat. It was too hard and they were too different.

Satisfied that she had tried her best, Daisy began to walk inside. Just then, she panicked and realized that she would get in trouble Daisy quickly grew worried about upsetting Peyton.

Daisy realized Delilah must have escaped under the fence. She frantically dug a hole to fit underneath the fence. She tried to squeeze under it. She almost fit. She just had to squeeze a little bit more. But, she was stuck once again.

Just then she heard Bone's laughter from inside. Bone was watching her try to fit through the fence and could see she was stuck.

"It's NOT funny, Bone. Stop laughing," Daisy shouted. She wiggled and wiggled, and eventually got out.

Daisy looked around and did not see Delilah. She ran through the forest. She sniffed and looked under every log.

Just then, in the distance, she saw something move by the river, and she sprinted over. As she got closer, she saw Delilah scratching at the bark of a tree trunk, trying to catch a bird.

Daisy raced towards her barking to get her attention.

"You can't leave the yard! What were you thinking? It's not always safe out here in the forest. You could get hurt or lost," Daisy shouted at Delilah.

"Well now you've done it. I almost caught that bird, but you scared it away," Delilah said angrily.

"We need to get back quickly before Peyton comes home and realizes we are gone," commanded Daisy.

"Again, with the worries. Who cares? You worry way too much. I'm staying. I'm having too much fun hunting," Delilah said defiantly.

Daisy was shocked. She couldn't understand Delilah and her cat lifestyle. This was the last straw; Daisy turned around to leave without Delilah. She will face the consequences from Peyton.

As Daisy was walking back to the house, she heard Delilah hissing loudly. She quickly turned around to see what was happening.

"MEEEOOOWWW, HISSSSS" Delilah was trying to scare a big, angry raccoon away.

The raccoon was not scared by her hissing. The raccoon was slowly approaching Delilah, its eyes fixed on her. Delilah did not know what more she could do to stop the raccoon. She was very frightened.

"WOOF, WOOF, WOOF, GURRR" Daisy came running towards the raccoon barking ferociously and showing her sharp teeth. Her loud and vicious barks stopped the raccoon in his tracks just in time. Daisy hoped he would turn and run away, but he did not.

Suddenly, Delilah spied a loose branch that was barely hanging onto the tree directly above the raccoon.

Like cats do best, Delilah swiftly climbed the tree while Daisy had the raccoon's attention.

Daisy continued to do what dogs do best and growled her scary bark. Together, they had the raccoon trapped.

Delilah knew what she had to do. She was afraid but knew she had to be brave to save herself and Daisy. She took a deep breath, lifted her paw, brought out her claws, and WHAM. She loosened the branch.

BOOM. The branch came tumbling out of the tree and BAM right in front of the raccoon, and scared him away in an instant.

Daisy lay down exhausted. Delilah quickly made her way down from the tree.

Delilah rubbed her nose up against Daisy's face and Daisy licked Delilah's face. They both laughed at their different displays of affection.

"Thank you for saving my life," Delilah purred.

"I was going to thank you for saving my life," Daisy woofed.

Delilah said "I could have never intimidated that raccoon like you. He was not frightened by my hissing."

"I could have never climbed the tree and knocked down the branch like you," said Daisy.

They then realized that it took their teamwork to stop the raccoon. Combining their different and unique qualities saved them. Together they made a wonderful team.

They walked home together, appreciating one another for their differences. In the coming days, they gave each other space to play the way both liked independently.

More importantly, they found ways they both could have fun together. Looking out the window, wrestling, chasing their tails, and drinking out of the toilet!

Despite their seemingly extreme differences, Daisy and Delilah became best friends.

Printed in the United States
by Baker & Taylor Publisher Services